Disney's
Beauty and the Beast

Once upon a time, in a faraway land, a young prince lived in a shining castle. Although he had everything a person could want, he had no love in his heart. One winter's night, an old woman came to the castle begging the prince for shelter from the cold. In return for this kindness, she offered him a single, perfect rose.

Disgusted by her rags, the prince sneered at the rose and turned the poor woman away.

"Do not be fooled by appearances," she warned him. "There is beauty to be found within all things."

Then, in a flash, the woman's ugliness melted away to reveal a lovely enchantress!

As punishment for his selfishness, the enchantress turned the prince into a hideous beast, the castle into a dark fortress, and the servants into household objects.

Before she left, she gave the prince two gifts: a magic mirror that allowed him to see the outside world, and the rose, which would only live until his twenty-first birthday.

"If you learn to love another and earn her love in return before the last petal of the rose has fallen," said the enchantress, "the spell will be broken. If not, you will remain a beast forever!"

A few years passed. One day, in a village not far from the castle, a young girl named Belle was crossing the town square. Belle loved to read, and as usual, she had her nose in a book.

The handsome but conceited Gaston watched her. Gaston admired Belle almost as much as he admired himself.

"She is the girl I am going to marry," he declared.

When Belle got home her father, Maurice, greeted her excitedly.

"I've just finished my latest invention!" he exclaimed. "I hope it works."

"Of course it will," Belle reassured him. "I'm sure it will win first prize at the fair!"

That afternoon Maurice hitched his invention to his horse, Philippe, and set off for the fair. But Maurice and Philippe became lost as they rode through the forest. Suddenly they heard the howling of wolves! The frightened horse reared up in alarm, sending poor Maurice flying through the air.

Maurice got up quickly and ran down a hillside
with the wolves snapping at his heels. He saw an
iron gate, slipped through it, and slammed it shut
just in time. He followed a path until he came to a
dark, forbidding castle. When no one answered his
knock, Maurice opened the creaking door and let
himself in.

No sooner was he inside than a strange thing happened. A candlestick bowed and began talking to him.

"Welcome, my good man!" said the candlestick.

Then a clock stepped out of the shadows and scolded the candlestick. "Lumiere, you know our master said not to let anyone in!"

"Oh, but now that he's here, Cogsworth," said Mrs. Potts, a talking teapot, "we must be kind to the old gentleman!" Her teacup son, Chip, agreed.

So they gave Maurice some tea, a bite to eat, and a chair to rest in.

Suddenly a dreadful beast burst into the room!

"A stranger!" he roared. "What are you doing here?"

"I just needed a place to stay," said Maurice timidly.

"I'll give you a place to stay!" shouted the Beast.
Then he scooped Maurice up in his hairy paws and
carried him off to the dungeon!

Back at the village, Belle was waiting for her father to return when Gaston came to ask for her hand in marriage. Belle tried to say no politely. "I really don't deserve you . . ." she started to say, but Gaston would not listen.

He had backed her up against the door when Belle reached for the doorknob. She opened the door and sent him sprawling down the steps into a giant puddle.

Later, Belle heard Philippe whinnying outside her window. "Where is Father?" she said to the horse. "Did something happen to him?"

Belle threw on a cloak and leaped onto Philippe's back. "Take me to Papa," she commanded.

Philippe sped through the forest until he came to the dark and uninviting castle. Belle saw her father's hat lying just inside the gate. She tied Philippe to a post and followed the path up to the castle.

"Papa, are you here?" cried Belle. She slowly pushed open the door of the castle and stepped inside. Lumiere, Cogsworth, Mrs. Potts, and Chip quietly followed Belle through the halls.

"Isn't she lovely?" whispered Mrs. Potts. "Perhaps she's the one who will break the spell."

Finally, Belle found her poor father locked away in a lonely cell. She was reaching out to touch his hand when the Beast suddenly appeared. Trembling with fright, Belle asked the Beast to let her father go.

"He is an old man," she begged. "Take me instead."

"Very well," said the Beast. "But you must promise to stay here forever."

"You have my word," replied Belle.

Then, before Belle could say a proper good-bye, the Beast dragged Maurice away and sent him home in an enchanted coach.

Soon the Beast returned for Belle.

"You may go anywhere you like," he said, as he showed her to her room, "but you must never go near the west wing."

Then the Beast shut the door. Belle was alone with Wardrobe, who was delighted to have a lovely young girl to dress.

Meanwhile, Maurice raced to the village tavern to get help.

"A hideous Beast has Belle locked up in his castle!" Maurice cried.

But Gaston and the villagers only laughed at him, so he left by himself to find Belle.

Later that night, Belle sneaked out of her room to eat and explore the castle. Cogsworth and Lumiere started to give Belle a tour, but she slipped away to see the forbidden west wing.

"I wonder what he's hiding there," she said.

When she came to the Beast's room, she found the enchanted rose under a bell jar. She was about to touch its soft petals when the Beast came charging towards her.

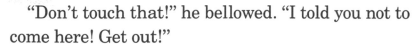

"Don't touch that!" he bellowed. "I told you not to come here! Get out!"

Belle ran from the room, down the stairs and out into the freezing night. She leaped onto Philippe and began to race him through the woods. She would not stay at the castle with the horrible beast, no matter what she had promised!

Suddenly, a pack of prowling wolves crept out from the darkness, their yellow eyes flashing in the night. Philippe reared up in fear, and Belle tumbled to the ground. But before the fierce creatures could pounce on her, the Beast came to Belle's rescue! The wolves attacked the Beast with their sharp teeth and claws, but he fought them off.

Belle mounted Philippe, and was about to make her escape, when she saw the injured Beast stagger and fall.

"I can't just leave him here," she said softly. "Help me get him back, Philippe." Together, Belle and the horse brought the Beast back to the castle.

Tenderly, Belle cleaned and bandaged the Beast's wounds.

"By the way," she said, "thank you for saving my life." Belle smiled at the Beast for the first time. Shyly, he smiled back.

In the days that followed, the Beast took Belle for walks in the garden, and he showed her his library. In return Belle began to teach him how to behave like a gentleman. Slowly, Belle and the Beast were becoming friends!

One night after dinner, the Beast bashfully led Belle to the ballroom. It wasn't long before they were waltzing gracefully across the dance floor.

"Are you happy here?" the Beast asked.

"Yes," said Belle. "If only I could see Papa . . ."

"There is a way," said the Beast, handing her the magic mirror. Belle gasped at the sight of her father, sick and lost in the forest.

"You must go to him," said the Beast sadly. "Take the mirror with you."

Belle found her father, and with the help of Philippe she got him home to bed. Soon, Maurice was well again.

Not long after, a strange man came to their door. Gaston and the villagers were with him.

"Gaston tells me that Maurice has been raving about a beast," the man told Belle. "I have come to take your father away to the asylum."

"Never!" replied Belle. "I will prove to you that my father is not crazy!" She held up the magic mirror so that everyone could see the Beast.

The villagers cried out in fright when they saw the Beast in the mirror.

"That Beast is dangerous!" Gaston shouted. "I say we go to the castle and get rid of him before he harms anyone!"

Belle tried to stop them, but it was no use.

Soon the angry crowd was storming the Beast's castle.

As Gaston ran upstairs to search for the Beast, the villagers broke into the dining hall. But the Beast's loyal servants were ready and waiting to attack. The villagers were no match for the pitchers, clocks, footstools and brushes. Soon they turned and fled from the castle in defeat.

Meanwhile, Gaston had found the Beast, and
chased him onto the roof. "Get up and fight!"
Gaston taunted.

But ever since Belle had left the castle, the Beast had lost interest in living. He didn't want to fight.

Gaston raised his club, ready to kill the Beast!

"Nooo!" Belle
cried from below.
She raced upstairs.

At the sight of
her, the Beast's
spirit returned and
he blocked the
club's blow. The
Beast grabbed Gas-
ton by the neck, but
he could no longer
find it in his heart
to hurt anyone. He
released Gaston,
unharmed.

As Belle arrived
and embraced the
Beast, Gaston
sneaked up from
behind. He stabbed
the beast in the
back!

Roaring in pain, the Beast struck out at Gaston.
Gaston took a step backward and lost his balance.
With a terrible scream, he fell from the roof and
was gone forever.

The Beast took a step toward Belle and then collapsed from his wounds.

"At least I got to see you one last time," said the Beast.

"You're going to be all right," said Belle through her tears. Then she whispered, "I love you."

In the Beast's room, Lumiere and Cogsworth watched in despair as the rose shed its last petal.

But then a sparkling, magical light surrounded the Beast. His paws became hands and feet, and the rest of his body was restored to its former handsomeness. Belle looked on in amazement as the Beast turned into a prince!

One by one the objects in the household became
human again. The spell was broken!

The Prince and Belle looked into each other's
eyes. As they kissed they knew that they would
live happily ever after!